There Are No Bears

An Ivy and Mack story

Written by Rebecca Colby

Illustrated by Gustavo Mazali

with Nuno Alexandre Vieira

Collins

What's in this story?

Listen and say 🎧1

blackberries

Download the audio at www.collins.co.uk/839694

forest

bear

Mack and Ivy went camping in the forest with Mum and Dad.

"Let's open the sleeping bags," said Ivy.

"Let's eat," said Mack.

"Let's put up the tent," said Dad.

"Oh no!" said Ivy. "Blackberries!"

"Don't you like blackberries?" asked Mum.

"Yes, I do," said Ivy. "But bears like blackberries, too! Are there bears in the forest?"

"Don't worry," said Dad. "There are no bears here."

That night, Mum and Dad cooked potatoes and beans on a fire.
"Look at the sky," said Mack. "The moon is so big!"

But Ivy looked at the tent.

"What's that?" she asked. "Is it a bear?"

"It *is* a bear," said Dad.

"But don't worry," said Dad. "It's only your teddy bear." Ivy felt a lot better.

After dinner, Mum washed the plates.
Dad put Ivy and Mack to bed.

"Let's read stories," said Mack. "I have a great book."

"OK," said Ivy.

Ivy was very quiet. She listened to Mack's story.

Then, Ivy heard a noise. "What was that?" she said to Mack.

"What?" he asked.

"Listen!" said Ivy

Ivy heard the noise again.

Mack heard it, too.

It was an animal. The animal moved!

"Look at that!" said Ivy. She pointed. Mack saw a big shape.

"The animal is eating! And it has big claws!" said Mack.

"Help! It's a bear!" said Ivy. "Dad! Mum!"

The animal came closer. It was very, very big.

Ivy looked at Mack. "What do we do?"

She called for Dad again. "Dad! Dad!"

"Where's Dad?" asked Ivy. "Did the hungry bear eat him?"

Mack put on his hat. "It's OK, Ivy!" he said. "Pick up your sleeping bag and come with me!"

Ivy was afraid. Mack was not.
"I can stop it," said Mack.
"Be careful!" said Ivy.

"What are you doing?" asked Mum.

"We stopped a bear!"

"A very hungry bear!" said Mack.

"That's not a hungry bear," said Mum.
She gave Ivy back her sleeping bag.
She was right ...

... It was a hungry Dad!

Ivy laughed, and Mack laughed.

"You can have one more biscuit, Dad," said Mack.

"We're having a bedtime biscuit party!" said Ivy.

Ivy and Mack sat by the fire with Mum and Dad. The night was beautiful and quiet. Then everyone heard a noise!

And Dad jumped!

"Don't worry, Dad! It's only a bird!" Ivy laughed. "There are no bears here!"

Picture dictionary

Listen and repeat

biscuit

camping

fire

moon

sky

sleeping bag

tent

1 Look and order the story

2 Listen and say

Collins

Published by Collins
An imprint of HarperCollins*Publishers*
Westerhill Road
Bishopbriggs
Glasgow
G64 2QT

HarperCollins*Publishers*
1st Floor, Watermarque Building
Ringsend Road
Dublin 4
Ireland

William Collins' dream of knowledge for all began with the publication of his first book in 1819.

A self-educated mill worker, he not only enriched millions of lives, but also founded a flourishing publishing house. Today, staying true to this spirit, Collins books are packed with inspiration, innovation and practical expertise. They place you at the centre of a world of possibility and give you exactly what you need to explore it.

10 9 8 7 6 5 4 3 2

ISBN 978-0-00-839694-7

Collins® and COBUILD® are registered trademarks of HarperCollins*Publishers* Limited

www.collins.co.uk/elt

British Library Cataloguing in Publication Data

A catalogue record for this publication is available from the British Library.

Author: Rebecca Colby
Lead illustrator: Gustavo Mazali (Beehive)
Copy illustrator: Nuno Alexandre Vieira (Beehive)
Series editor: Rebecca Adlard
Commissioning editor: Zoë Clarke
Publishing manager: Lisa Todd
Product managers: Jennifer Hall and Caroline Green
In-house editor: Alma Puts Keren
Project manager: Emily Hooton
Editor: Deborah Friedland
Proofreaders: Natalie Murray and Michael Lamb
Cover designer: Kevin Robbins
Typesetter: 2Hoots Publishing Services Ltd
Audio produced by id audio, London
Reading guide author: Julie Penn
Production controller: Rachel Weaver
Printed and bound by: GPS Group, Slovenia

MIX
Paper from
responsible sources
FSC™ C007454

This book is produced from independently certified FSC™ paper to ensure responsible forest management.

For more information visit: **www.harpercollins.co.uk/green**

Download the audio for this book and a reading guide for parents and teachers at www.collins.co.uk/839694